The Big Princess

Taro Miura

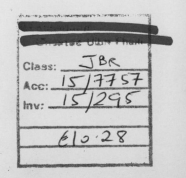

WALKER BOOKS
AND SUBSIDIARIES
LONDON · BOSTON · SYDNEY · AUCKLAND

Once upon a time in a land far, far away,
there lived a king and queen.
The king and queen had no children of
their own, but they had a beautiful garden,
full of all kinds of flowers. It was their pride
and joy and each blossom was tended
with the greatest love and care.

One night, a white bird came to the king
in his dreams. It had a message for him.
"You and your queen will be sent a child,"
the bird said. "Go to your garden when
you wake. There, among your flowers, you
will find a princess, as sweet and charming
as your most cherished blossom.
But be warned: the princess is under a spell . . .
If you are able to break this spell, the princess
will become your true daughter."
"And if I cannot break it?" asked the king.
"Then your kingdom will fall to ruins and
be lost forever."

When morning came, the king
remembered his strange dream.
Could it be true? He leaped out of bed
and ran to the garden.

He searched high and low, but the
princess was nowhere to be found.
It was just a dream, after all,
thought the king, his heart heavy.
But then he heard a little voice:
"Your Majesty."
The king turned around, and there,
perched on a dew-speckled leaf,
was a lovely, tiny princess.

Very carefully, the king placed
the princess in his hand
and carried her to his queen.

When the queen saw the tiny princess, she was overjoyed.

Then the king told her about his dream.

What spell could the princess be under? And if they
failed to break it, what would happen to their kingdom?

But the more the queen looked at the perfectly
lovely little princess, the more she could not
believe that someone so precious
would ever bring them harm.

The happy queen wanted to prepare a bed

for her tiny princess right away.

But what kind of bed would she sleep in?

She was so little!

Then the queen had an idea.

She pulled a feather out of her crown,

and laid the princess on it.

The tiny princess floated up and down

on her fluffy, feathery bed.

The next morning, to everyone's surprise,

the princess had grown, and the feather bed

had already become too small for her.

So the queen found . . .

a little ring box.

The sparkly box was the perfect bed

for a little gem of a princess.

But the next day - oh no! -

the princess had grown again!

And now, her ring box bed

was too small for her.

The queen looked again.

And this time, she found . . .

her favourite teacup.
She filled it with soft, fluffy cotton
and, well, what a wonderful bed
it was for the little princess!

Until the next day, when the
little princess had grown . . . again!
Now, even the teacup bed was too small
for her! So, the queen searched
for a new bed once more and found . . .

a cuddly teddy bear.

Teddy bear's tummy was soft and warm,

and the little princess was so very cosy

and so very happy.

But to everyone's astonishment,

as the days went by . . .

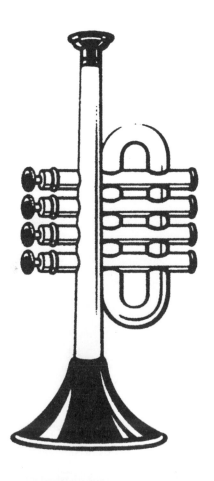

the princess kept growing and growing
until, at last, she was even too big
for a child's bed! In fact, every single bed
made for the little princess became
much too small by the very next day.

No one had ever heard
of such a thing.
The princess kept growing
bigger and BIGGER.
Soon, she was even taller
than the king and the queen.
They were beside themselves
with worry –
just how much more was
she going to grow?

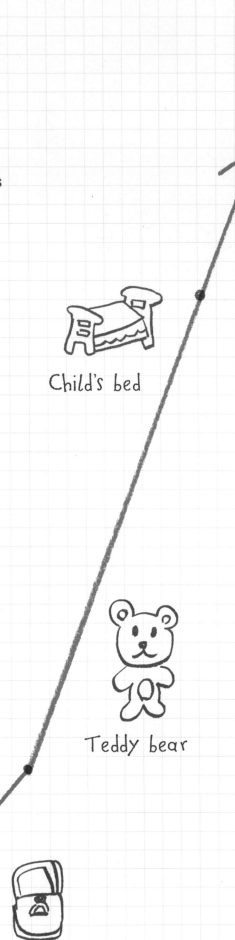

Child's bed

Teddy bear

Teacup

Ring box

Feather

Oh, no!

The poor princess was now almost
too big for the castle itself.
She cried and cried and her giant tears
fell to the ground, flooding the castle.

Then at last the king remembered his dream –
this must be the dangerous spell the white
bird had warned him about. He knew he had
to break it. But how?
Together the king and queen tried everything
they could to break the spell.
But no matter what they did, nothing worked.

The king had no choice: he had to move

his princess to the tallest tower in the castle.

Even then, she kept growing . . .

bigger and bigger and bigger . . .

the tower started to bulge, the walls

began to crack and –

BOOM!

The top of the tower burst open.

The king wrung his hands in despair.

I can't give up, he thought,

I have to save my daughter!

And with hope in his heart,

he looked up at his giant princess.

And that's when he saw it.

There, in the tower window!

It was the princess's belly button,

and something was hidden inside it . . .

something shiny.

"What on earth is that?" cried the king.

He had a ladder brought at once,

and began to climb the crumbling tower.

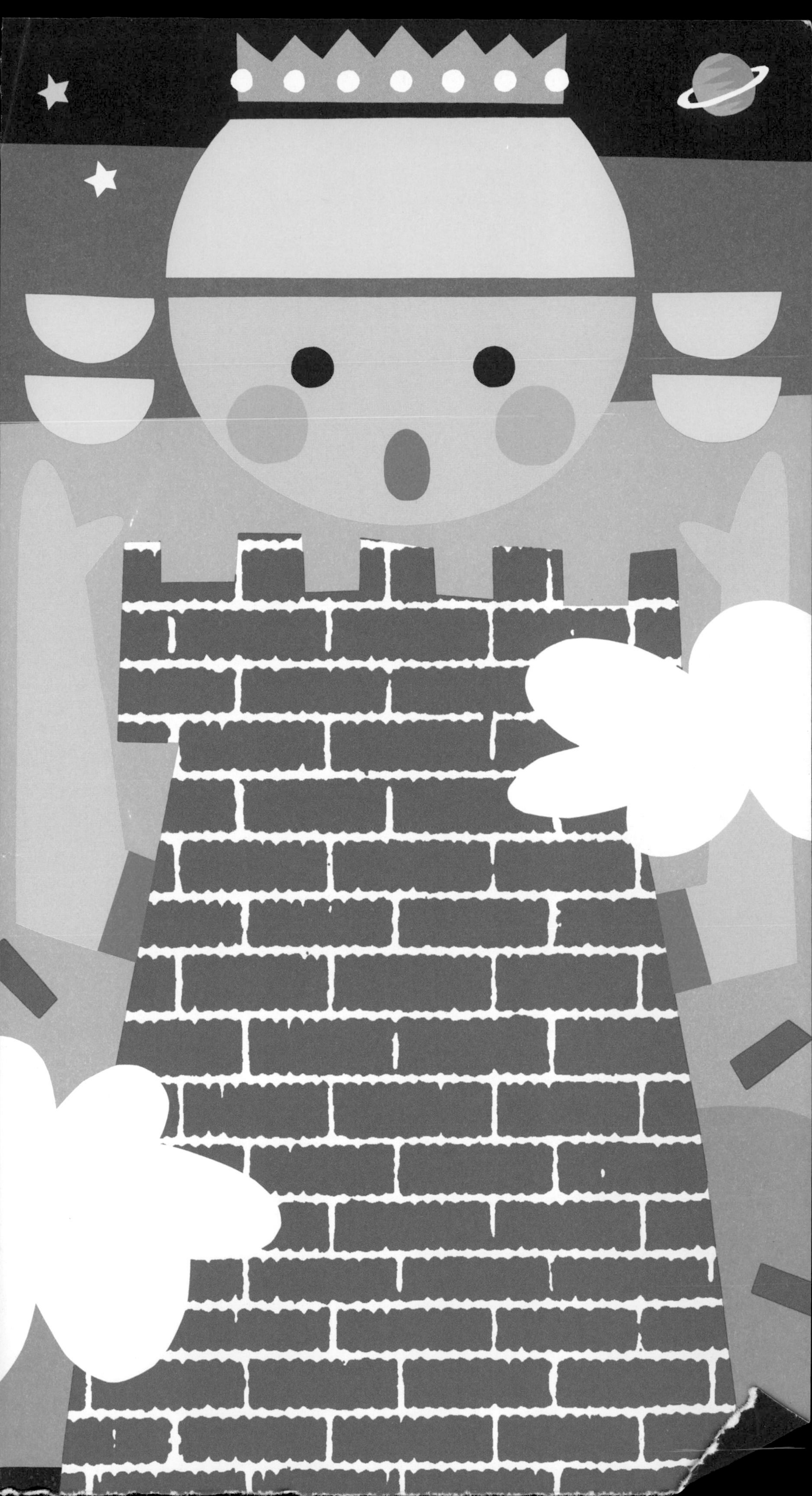

When the king got to the tower window,

he reached out for the shiny object.

As he did, he tickled the princess's tummy.

The princess giggled, and the tower

rocked back and forth.

Any moment now, the tower was going to fall down.

Then there was a

POP!

And out of the princess's belly button dropped

a shiny black seed, right into the king's hand.

Guess what happened next?

The princess suddenly grew smaller and smaller!

"The spell is broken!" cried the king,

and he felt light with all the joy in his heart.

That's how the king broke the spell

and he and his family lived happily ever after.

And though the princess was now a lot smaller,
she was still a *little* bigger than the average princess.

And what of the shiny black seed?

Well, it was planted in the castle garden, where

it soon grew into a field of giant, beautiful flowers.

The World's Biggest Sunflower

This year in FlowerLand, a big sunflower variety, BIG PRINCESS, is our original shot up to touch the sky. True to its name, the flower grew to 8.84 meters (measured previous world building record in 2009) by 0.01 three stories surpassed the in Germany to bring crown to BIG PRINCESS.

The people in the kingdom called the flowers 'Big Princesses'. And to this day they tend them with much love and care.